SIR PIGGLESWORTH ADVENTURE SERIES

Sir Pigglesworth's First Adventure

By JoAnn Wagner and Sara Dean
Illustrations by David Darchicourt

This book is a work of fiction. Some names, characters, places, and incidents are the product of the creator's imagination or are used fictitiously.

All trademarked names are the exclusive property of their respective owners and not of the author.

Sir Pigglesworth Publishing, Inc.
1515 N. Town East Blvd, Suite 138-118
Mesquite, TX 75150

Revised October 2016
Printed in China
10 9 8 7 6 5 4 3 2

The publisher is not responsible for websites (or their content) that are not owned by the publisher.

Paperback: ISBN 978-1-68055-051-1
Hardcover: ISBN 978-1-68055-052-8
EBook: ISBN 978-1-68055-053-5

www.sirpigglesworth.com

This series is dedicated to the people of New Community Church, Mesquite, TX

Special recognition to Pastors Chris Railey and Aaron Escamilla whose flying pig gave wings to my idea.

Heartfelt thanks to Sara Dean and David Darchicourt for their hard work and dedication to making my dream a reality.

Many thanks to my family and friends for their support and encouragement for me to pursue my dream.

JoAnn Wagner
September 2014

After being knighted by Queen Alexandra for acts of bravery, Sir Pigglesworth was commissioned as her emissary to travel around the world to spread cheer and smiles with all the children he meets.

Join Sir Pigglesworth as he leads you on a merry romp throughout each city he visits!

He will learn about the culture and history everywhere he visits and share this information with all children of the world.

First stop...LONDON!!

Get ready to learn and laugh, and love "Sir Pigglesworth" as he travels the world in search of fun and adventure!

Sir Pigglesworth's First Adventure

partures
t 4506 on schedule
1216 on schedule
3600 on schedule
002 on schedule
876 on schedule
Welcome
Heathro
FUEL

Chapter 1

The plane ride had taken far too long for such a small pig.

After many hours of sitting still, little Sir Pigglesworth excitedly popped out of his seat and ran off the plane.

Sir Pigglesworth had never been in an airport before.

A trip to London with his parents, the Duke and Duchess of Pigglesworth, was a very big treat for him!

DAILY
NEWS
Coffee
Shoppe
Shiney
Shoe
DAILY NEWS
THE
TOWER
OF
LONDON
TIMES
TOURS
OF
LONDON

The young 5 year-old pig was so amazed by everything around him that he forgot something very important.

He forgot to wait for his parents!

But who could blame him? There were so many interesting sights all around to catch his eye!

Oh, I'm sure they are just a few steps behind me, he thought.

PRETZ
SPALDING

Sir Pigglesworth walked past a gift shop filled with toys.

He really liked the dinosaur, cars, and the baseball glove he saw, but not the big yellow bows sitting next to the glove.

The bows made him think of his cousin, Andrea. She loved to wear bows on her hair. She even wore a big bow on her curly tail!

Sir Pigglesworth thought Andrea looked a little silly, but Andrea always said, "My bows and I are beautiful!"

As he was thinking of Andrea and her bows, a yummy smell distracted him.

Gifts
Gifts

He turned around to see a case of freshly baked pretzels.

How delicious those warm pretzels smelled! His tummy growled.

Sir Pigglesworth realized he was hungry after his long plane ride.

As he stepped closer to the case, he was distracted again by a very colorful sight!

He couldn't take his eyes off of a man with blue hair that stood straight up like spikes on top of his head.

Sir Pigglesworth had never seen anything like it!

He wondered what he would look like if he colored his ears and tail blue.

The thought made him laugh.

He was still laughing as he walked on, imagining the look on Andrea's face if she saw him with blue ears and a blue tail.

He thought she would be so shocked that her bows would fly right off. The thought made him laugh even harder.

?
BOUNCE!
WAM!

Chapter 2

Sir Pigglesworth was so lost in his own thoughts that he didn't watch where he was going.

The next thing he knew he felt a BUMP and then a THUMP as he fell backwards on his RUMP!

Sir Pigglesworth blinked in confusion and looked up.

A tall man turned around and asked, "Are you okay?"

The man bent down and helped Sir Pigglesworth stand up.

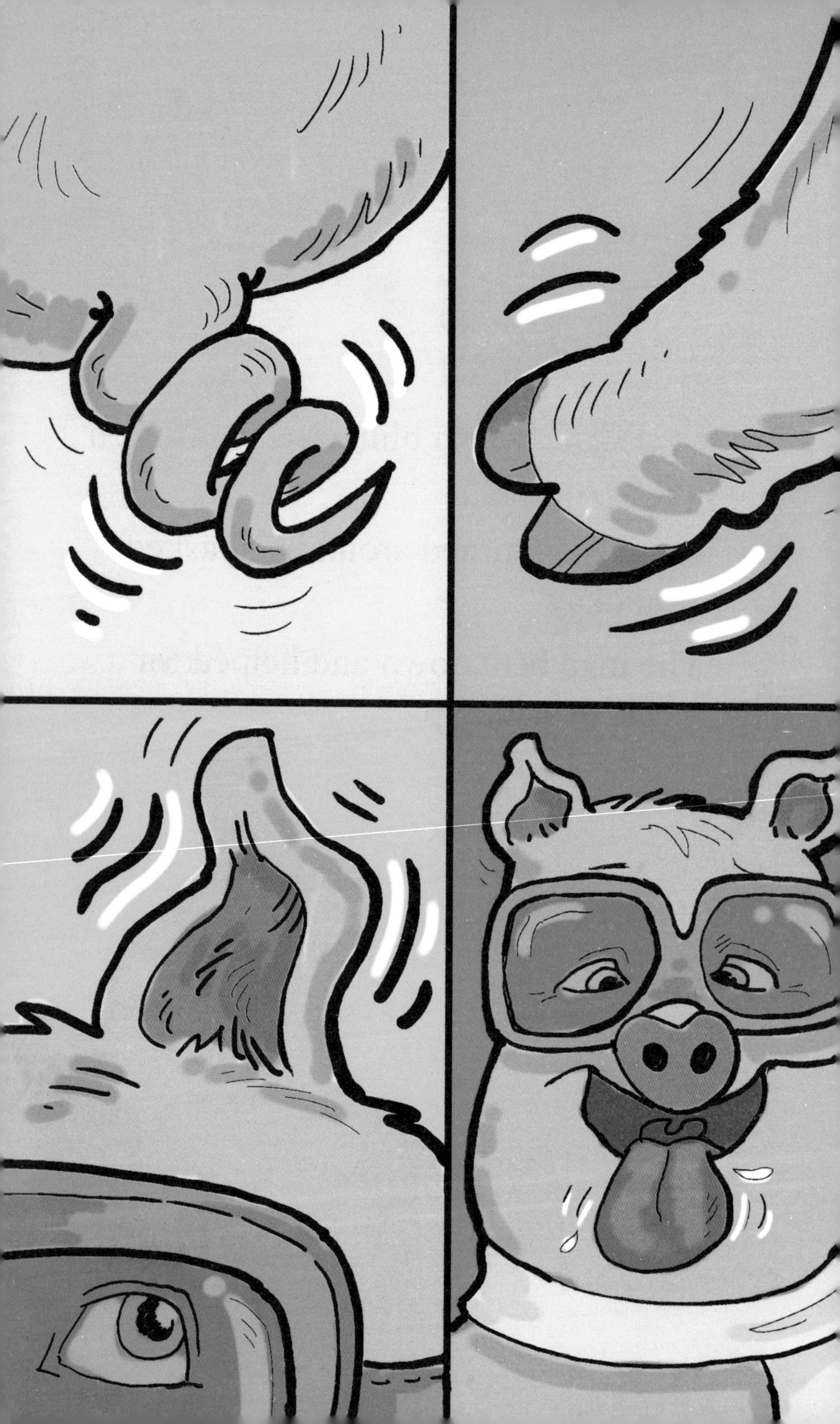

Sir Pigglesworth waggled his tail and each of his hooves, and wiggled each ear.

Then he looked cross-eyed at his tongue which he had stuck out as far as it would go.

"Yep," he said at last. "Looks like I'm just fine."

"I'm glad to hear that," the man said with a laugh.

"My name is Bill and this is my wife, JoAnn," he said pointing to the lady standing next to him.

12:45
12:55
1:05
1:30
1:45

“It’s a pleasure to meet you. I’m Sir Pigglesworth,” the small pig said.

He reached out one hoof to shake the man’s hand.

SCRATCH

“Oh, he’s so polite!” JoAnn said with a big smile. “And he’s so cute!”

She bent down and scratched behind his ear.

Sir Pigglesworth loved to be scratched behind his ears.

He instantly liked JoAnn.

“So tell me,” Bill asked. “What is a small pig like you doing in a big place like this all by yourself?”

“Oh, I’m not alone,” Sir Pigglesworth told him. “I’m here with my mom and dad.”

“They’re right over here,” he said as he looked behind him. “Or...over...here?”

Sir Pigglesworth nervously looked from side to side. “Well...they were here a minute ago…I think.”

He suddenly realized he was lost.

“Don’t worry,” JoAnn said. “We’ll help you find your parents.”

Depar
12:45 flight 45
12:55 flight 1
1:05 flight
1:30 flight
1:45 fligh

Since they were the only royal pig family at the airport, the Duke and Duchess of Pigglesworth were pretty easy to find.

Many people noticed the pig couple who wore fancy clothes and jewelry.

Even more people heard them shouting out, “Sir Pigglesworth, Sir Pigglesworth! Where are you?”

The Duke and Duchess spotted their little pig and quickly ran to give him hugs and kisses.

Sir Pigglesworth was so happy to be back with his mom and dad!

"It's time for us to get our luggage and go to our hotel," said JoAnn.

"You be safe, little pig, and be sure to stay close to your mom and dad," she told Sir Pigglesworth.

"I will. Thank you for helping me find my parents." He waved goodbye to his new friends as they walked away.

Sir Pigglesworth felt a little sad when he realized he would probably never see them again.

Chapter 3

That night, Sir Pigglesworth and his family went to a restaurant for dinner.

He peeked over at one of the tables and his heart skipped a beat.

Sir Pigglesworth was surprised to see his friends Bill and JoAnn!

Bill and JoAnn spotted Sir Pigglesworth and his family and they waved. Everyone was happy to see each other again.

“Can we sit with them, please, please?” Sir Pigglesworth begged his parents.

Sir Pigglesworth was excited to spend time with his new friends.

His parents enjoyed getting to know Bill and JoAnn.

Even though pigs and people are very different, they found that they had a lot in common with each other.

JoAnn and the Duchess shared stories about their travels; Bill and the Duke talked about their favorite sports teams.

Sir Pigglesworth was very happy that everyone was getting along so well.

The adults were so busy talking no one noticed that he gobbled up his dessert before he ate his dinner.

After dinner, they all said goodbye again and promised they would keep in touch with each other.

Wibbly's
Fish & Chips
Wibbly's
Fish & Chips
TELE

Chapter 4

Sir Pigglesworth and his family went sightseeing in London the next day.

First they visited Buckingham Palace where the Queen lives.

They took a tour of the palace and watched the changing of the guard ceremony. The guards protect the palace and the Queen.

Next they toured Parliament which is where the government writes the laws of the country.

Afterwards, they stood on a long line to go into Westminster Abbey.

It was the most beautiful church Sir Pigglesworth had ever seen. He was amazed by how big it was!

After they finished the tour, Sir Pigglesworth and his mom and dad took a boat ride down the Thames River. The boat sailed right under the Tower Bridge.

He learned that the bridge has stood over the river since 1894, and that it is the only bridge on the river that can be raised to let big boats sail under it.

He thought how awesome it would be to see that.

He wished a big boat would come by right then so he could see the bridge raise up and down.

Back on land after the boat ride, the family rode on a red double-decker bus.

Sir Pigglesworth was excited to sit outside on the top of the bus. With so many sights to see, he had a hard time sitting still!

They rode the bus right up to the London Eye. It is a very tall ferris wheel that had been built to help London celebrate the new century.

It is so tall you can see all of London from the very top.

Everyone on the ground looked like ants to him.

It was a little scary to the small piglet to be so high up in the sky!

COMIC

Chapter 5

Before he knew it, it was time to go home. Sir Pigglesworth was sad that he did not see Bill and JoAnn again.

They were not home long before his parents said that they were leaving for their next trip.

They planned for Sir Pigglesworth to stay at home with his grandmother.

“We will only be gone for a few days,” his mom told him. “You be a good little pig for grandma.”

She kissed him on his snout and went to pack her suitcase.

But the mischievous little piglet had a different plan.

"I'm going with them," he whispered.

With his mind made up, he packed his small suitcase and took off for the airport.

GATE 6
American Airlines
Flight 208
Vancouver
GATE 7
American Airlines
Flight 605
Dallas
BOARDING
FLY!
BOARDING
TWA
AA
DUDE

Sir Pigglesworth didn't know which plane his parents were going to board.

So he played a guessing game of 'eeny -meeny-miney-mo' to choose one.

"And you are it," he said pointing at a line nearby getting ready to board a plane.

There was a large sign above the entrance to Gate 7 that read, 'American Airlines, Flight 605, Dallas'.

I guess that's the right one, he thought and headed to the gate.

BOARDING

Sir Pigglesworth didn't have a ticket, so he couldn't board the plane like everyone else.

Instead, he hid in a woman's carry-on bag as she was waiting to get on the plane.

It turned out her bag was too big to carry on, so it was sent to the luggage cargo hold in the very bottom of the plane.

Once inside the luggage area on the plane, he wiggled out of the bag and lay among the suitcases that were bouncing all around him.

It was a bumpy ride, and it very cold.

Sir Pigglesworth wished he had found a better hiding place.

AA FLIGHT 605
Pick-Up
THIS END UP

After a long time the plane landed. Sir Pigglesworth was tossed out onto a conveyor belt with all the suitcases.

It was a very fast slide down the ramp to the carousel and his stomach flip-flopped with fright!

He was in a daze as the carousel was slowly moving in a circle.

Around and around went the conveyor belt, like a giant merry-go-round of suitcases instead of horses.

As he rode on the conveyor belt, Sir Pigglesworth tried to find his mom and dad in the crowd.

He was sure that they would be happy and surprised to see him there!

He wished they would get here soon because he was getting dizzy from going around and around.

Chapter 6

Much to his surprise it wasn't his mom and dad who showed up. It was his friends Bill and JoAnn!

"What are you doing here?" they all asked at the same time.

"I'm waiting to surprise my mom and dad. They think I'm at home with my grandmother."

"But I'm here to join them in Vancouver," said Sir Pigglesworth.

Bill and JoAnn looked at each other then back at Sir Pigglesworth.

“You’re not in Vancouver,” Bill said. “You’re in Dallas, Texas.”

Sir Pigglesworth looked a little green. He felt sick.

He wasn’t sure if he felt sick because he was lost again or because the luggage carousel was going around and around in a big circle, making him feel dizzy.

JoAnn noticed their little friend's color and gently lifted him off the belt.

"Don't worry," she said softly. "We live here. We're going to take you home with us while we figure out where to find your mom and dad."

"You live in the airport?" Sir Pigglesworth asked.

JoAnn laughed. "No," she said. "We live in Dallas."

"You're going to like being here while we decide where to look for your parents. Dallas is a beautiful city."

SCRATCH!

“How will I find my mom and dad if I stay here?” Sir Pigglesworth asked.

JoAnn looked at Bill. He knew just what she was thinking.

“We’re going to help you find your parents,” Bill said.

“You’re going to help me find them?” Sir Pigglesworth asked, thinking about all of the ear scratches he would get from JoAnn between Dallas and Vancouver.

Welcome to Dallas
PARK-N-TRAVEL

“Yes,” JoAnn said. “We’ll think of it as an adventure.”

“An adventure!” Sir Pigglesworth repeated. “I like that!”

“First we’ll call your grandmother to let her know you’re safe,” said JoAnn.

And off they went to start their adventure together.

THE END

Join us for Book 2
Sir Pigglesworth's Adventures in Vancouver

For information on other "*Sir Pigglesworth Adventure Series*" books, please visit:
www.SirPigglesworth.com

Meet the Author:
www.JoAnnWagner.com
https://www.facebook.com/joann.g.wagner
Twitter: @AuthorJoJo

Books available at
www.SirPigglesworth.com
www.BarnesandNoble.com
www.Amazon.com

Bulk purchases available at:
www.SirPigglesworthPublishing.com

For free cartoons delivered daily to your email visit: www.SharingSmilesAroundTheWorld.com